Takwe À Taamba

DISCLAIMER

Takwe À Taamba

The Wise vs. The Idiots

Labah Nformi

Contents

FOREWORD

Takwe and Taamba are the main characters in trickster tales of Wimbum people. The Wimbum people are in Nkambe Central and Ndu Sub Divisions of the Donga-Mantung Division of the North West Region of Cameroon in West Africa. The language spoken by the Wimbum people is Limbum.

I have just tried to retell the folktales as they were told to us. I am simply a translator of the oral tales into English. I owe everything to my mother, Ancella Mutab Kijah Ndop, who narrated these stories and more to us over and over again, at the fireside for warm, cohesion, family communion.These used to be key moments of entertainment, fun and jokes from our parents and any elder gifted in the art of storytelling. The oral rendition was more lively, dynamic and so much improvisation on the part of the narrator and, especially with a participatory audience, listeners humming or singing the chorus, handclapping, foot stamping. Our imaginations were expanded and stretched beyond the realm of the real and surreal and our curiosity to learn and know more was unbridled,

The first audience for my own folktales were my own children: Cheche, Tamfu, Nyugab, Nyufersii, Webchu and Ntunyu away from home wanted these stories written. I tried to satisfy them by narrating these folktales in (Limbum) our mother tongue and did translations into English a few years ago with much difficulty and much improvisation, missing the authenticity and flavor of the songs. I decided to publish them this time to enable them and many others who didn't have the opportunity to learn these stories at the fireside like children like us who grew up in a typical Wimbum village and also to pay homage to my (our storyteller) mother who passed away last year August 15, 2021.

Presently many stories about Takwe and Taamba can be found in literary journals in schools and students' magazines, pamphlets in English, Limbum and other Languages. Takwe and Taamba are no longer animal characters with human features who play tricks, and distort the rules as we knew them as kids. In a derogatory sense, in the Limbum language, Takwe stands for any person (character) who is cunning, trickish, anyone envious, or anyone who uses his wisdom for selfish and egoistic purposes. In a typical rural setting, anyone who works against the communal interest, anyone who wants to succeed alone or reap where he has not sown. Taamba, on the other hand, literally is a person (character) who is not clever, gullible, or easily manipulated. It is for this reason that I captioned this collection; *Takwe and Taamba -The Wise Vs the Idiots. Though the "Wise" claim a monopoly over wisdom, they can still learn from the Idiots"*

1. Excreta spoiled Taamba's marriage

A Long time ago,

Taamba was wooing a pretty damsel

Takwe, his best friend, was always invited

to accompany him to all his in-laws.

Takwe was a sweet talker who could

entertain everyone on all occasions.

His presence everywhere put similes

on all faces; the young and the old.

Taamba, his close friend who was not

so eloquent; needed such a companion

when he was wooing the woman of his life.

Taamba was very brave and courageous,

hard-working, friendly and very generous.

These are some of the qualities that made

him the most admirable and top suitor.

His happiest moments were when he was

chasing animals up and down the slopes

up and down the bushy and rough valleys

between hanging impenetrable rocks

slamming them into hollow caves where

Takwe and other weak hunters picked

and squeezed the bleeding animals to put

in hunting bags slung across their shoulders

Taamba did the greatest job and took

the greatest risk hunting;

But accepted whatever share

was given to him at the end.

Takwe didn't have the weight, height and size

Of Taamba, his inseparable companion.

The presence of Taamba always overshadowed

Takwe's presence in all occasions but wherever

the imposing presence of Taamba's shadow

was seen, everyone knew that Takwe's shadow

was lingering somewhere around the corner.

Many believe these two buddies were born the same

day; one in the day and the other at night.

Tamba's engagement with this pretty damsel was

the talk of the village and all neighboring villagers.

His admirers considered it a perfect match

that would define and refine an ideal marriage.

A young, pretty, charming damsel

to a brave, courageous,hard-working hunter.

They said that marriage would be the best

because beauty had matched with bravery

and courage for the first time in the village.

It was an amorous engagement; the new moon

was leaning to the left, a charming lovely moon

when left-handed like Taamba progress and gain

more favors; he struck down more games this moon.

Taamba's admirers were worried about the presence of Takwe

in all visits and negotiations with the father and mother in law.

Takwe was notorious for turning villagers' good luck to bad luck

With his honey-coated tongue; he had duped almost all villagers.

Many villagers duped like Taamba still sorted his advice and services.

His admirers were worried because the hearts and minds of
tender lovers

Quiver and shiver like chicks when they see the shadow of a
hawk.

Takwe and Taamba went to the village of their would-be in-laws

Taamba put on his best appearance and behavior and didn't
talk much

Takwe did much of the talking; animating the host with fun and
jokes

The father and mother in law didn't cease laughing throughout
their visit

They openly praised Takwe and, most of the time, forgot about
Taamba.

Taamba ate his supper greedily and licked the bowls with his
tongue.

"Hard working suitors eat well because they can provide enough"

Takwe had advised him to do so and went on

"Only lazy suitors eat lightly because they can't provide enough"

Taamba cracked the bones, sucked the marrow and asked
for more

Really he had more because Takwe ate lightly and didn't crack
the bones

"Good eaters are also good drinkers" Takwe told his friend

So Taamba gulped gourds of wine to the dregs and asked for
more.

. . .

Takwe sipped his wine and entertained the host with more riddles and jokes.

To the admiration of Taamba's fiancée who, according to tradition, didn't talk much.

Taamba went to bed without saying good night to his fiancée and in-laws.

In the morning Taamba's mat was dripping with urine and feces.

He was smeared in feces from head to toe like a masquerade.

Takwe and Taamba tried to cover up and clean the mess, but it was too late

The fiancée who came to tell them that breakfast was ready; hesitated

"Hoock! Hoock! Hoock! was heard as she held her ribs and regurgitated

The fiancée, one day on their second visit, heard Takwe singing:

The love between beauty and brute force can't be true

The love between hunters and farmers can't go through

The love between water and fire can't be defined

The love between the idiots and the wise meets a dead end

Takwe had interceded with the in-laws to give Taamba a second chance

Taamba worked extra hard because of his strength, bravery and brute force

He caught bigger games, had bigger calabashes of palm oil and wine

To prove that he deserved the first position in the chain of lucky suitors

He built new barns and granaries and renovated the old ones

He ate well, drank well, spoke well and behaved well and slept well

But still messed up his bed and his mat dripped with urine and feces again.

He was smeared in feces like a crawling baby left in its mess the whole night.

Takwe who slept with him in the same room, tried another cover-up

But the fiancée knocked at the door; hit by the smell; she hesitated

HooK! Hoo! HooK! was heard as she held her ribs and regurgitated

Taamba was hurriedly rushed out to the stream and back to his village

Takwe, an intercessor remained behind and pleaded for a third chance

Takwe's honey coated tongue obtained it but with much difficulty

Taamba worked extra hard because of his strength, bravery and brute force

He caught the biggest games, had the biggest calabashes of palm oil and wine

To prove that he still deserved the top position in the chain of lucky suitors

He ate better, drank better, spoke better and behaved better and slept better

But still messed up the bamboo bed and his mat dripped with feces and urine

He was smeared in feces like a puppy pulled out of a pit latrine.

The fiancée didn't have a tongue to openly curse Taamba openly

because no bride to-be has never done so in the grassland

The father in-law swallowed his tongue and sealed his lips

because no father-in-law had ever let his tongue loose like a woman

But the mother in- law's throat could not swallow the pus any longer

For the first time in the land, a mother-in-law poured curses

on a soon-to-be son-in-law in the presence of onlookers.

I've never seen a son-in-law

Who brought himself so low

I thought your love would grow

But you've made tears flow

Like tears of a foul waterfall

Who says it's not your fault!

Taamba you're a disgrace

You'll live forever on grass

Like a goat, chew the cud and grow horns

Curse your stars and the day you were born.

Taamba fled from his in-laws and was ashamed to go back to his village

spent a whole hunting season wandering and wondering why.

He put his anger, frustration and energy into hunting more animals

And blocked his ears from the hearsay that his close friend

Takwe was engaged to marry the damsel of his life.

Takwe had succeeded in winning the heart of Taamba's fiancée

Taamba's hard work was now replaced with Takwe's nice stories

The big gifts that Taamba brought were replaced with big riddles and jokes

And all arrangements had been made for the wedding after the harvest season

Takwe was heard by the father and mother in-law on their farm loitering and reaping

where he didn't sow; like birds of the sky and singing like a weaver bird on a sunny day

Where idiots fail;

the wise succeed.

Where would I have had a wife?

Thanks to my urine and excreta.

Where Idiots like Taamba fail;

the wise like me succeed.

Where idiots fail ;

the wise succeed.

Where would I have had a wife?

Thanks to my urine and excreta.

The villagers who were anxiously waiting for the wedding

one day they heard a song that no one had ever heard

The father and mother-in-law were strolling and singing

Looking frustrated and dejected with hands on their heads

Pleading to all wise villagers to join in singing the chorus

So that they all, as one, can destroy the trickster virus

Shame, shame, shame ooh

what we do in the dark

Can come to light one day

Shame, shame, shame ooh

Where a brave, stupid in-law like Taamba failed

A lazy, trickster in -law like Takwe can't succeed

Only an idiot can solemnize such a marriage "

Shame, shame, shame ooh

2. Taamba, the first thief in a village

A long time ago;

A village in the grass field was ruled by a wise chief

The villagers were hard-working, law abiding and honest

For many years the villagers have never heard of or seen a thief

But one hunting season, they welcomed two honorable guests

Takwe and Taamba, two inseparable hunters from the Midwest

One was very brave, courageous, hard-working but very foolish

The other was very mean, lazy, trickish,a talkative but very selfish

The villagers enjoyed working hard just like they enjoyed their delicious meals

Their doors were opened to all, even to strangers, at all times; night and day

The villagers shared their meals with everyone just like they shared their smiles.

The generous villagers gave Takwe and Taamba a comfortable place to stay.

There was much fun, riddles, songs and dance in the village arena, open to all.

The villagers were generous, so they celebrated moonlit nights like birthdays

The wise chief stored their surplus yields in underground barns in a big hall

So, the villagers had very few life challenges but never problems from thieves.

Taamba immediately joined the growing number of hunters.

He taught timid villagers hunting skills that made them brave

The villagers saw him as a great companion and a great fighter

Taamba made them know that those who hunt can never starve

The chief encouraged his subjects to learn his hunting skills

The once timid hunters could camouflage in valleys and hills;

And caught many big games they couldn't catch with archaic skills.

Takwe stayed home and narrated his successful hunting adventures

He lectured the villagers on the dos and don'ts of hunting traditions

And helped the wise chief in the conservation of his village treasures

And warned quarrelsome hunters of the ills of unnecessary competition

Which made so many hunting outings to be rough and unpredictable

He advised the chief to be strict and cut lazy and idle hunters' ration

To compensate those like him who have made hunting enjoyable.

Taamba was promoted to head the Hunting Committee

WhileTakwe was promoted to lead the Sharing Committee

Taamba killed more animals and showed his hidden skills

Takwe collected the juiciest portions of every game killed

And reserved to share equally between him and the chief

No villager dared, challenged or questioned Takwe's mischief

Because he had promised heady hunters positions of sub-chiefs

And those who opposed him were seen as crooks and thieves

Takwe raised an alarm a season later that things were not normal

Hens started squawking anyhow and cockerels took over from roosters

For the first time, a brave hunter and his dogs were chased by an animal

When this happened, Takwe started treating some hunters like bastards

And said they were greedy hunters who starved dogs and hid some animals

Caught by the dogs to share in the caves in disrespect of the hunting rosters

Takwe raised an alarm that the uninitiated were eating gizzards

And idle children were frying and boiling eggs in the afternoon

He also said some lazy hunters were hunting and eating lizards

A few families could boost a chicken and many had none

Hawks snatched fowls and goats were devoured by wolves

Lack of trust was installed and many preferred hunting alone

But the chief was so cautious talking about crooks and thieves

Takwe praised those who work less and take time to rest

Like him because it is not hard work that can stop hunger

He said since the chief rewarded him, he is doing his best

He didn't stop the story time, fun and dance because of his anger

Since the farmers and hunters no longer sit and eat together

It was not necessary for husbands to corporate with their wives

Because partners stealthily do certain things and no one bothered

Why; still, the wise chief refused to talk about crooks and thieves

.   .   .

The wise chief one evening was talking aloud to himself

"Simplicity that united my subjects has given way to duplicity

Hard Work that united my subjects has given way to idleness

The generosity that united my subjects has given way to stinginess

The beauty of the heart, body, mind and soul has given way to ugliness

Smartness that was at the core of the village has given to clumsiness"

All that the wise chief did was going down the drain

For the first time, his advisers challenged his reign

His farmers were more and more losing their brains

Because it was hard every season to have regular rains

So the hungry, angry farmers were losing their grains

To weevils and tubers were as if they were soaked in brine

So, the villagers asked Takwe to pull them out of the drain

Takwe took upon himself the job of an instructor

"A thief shivers and trembles when questioned"

Takwe told the council of elders.

"A thief may urinate on himself when questioned"

Takwe added

"A thief may refuse to eat corn fufu though hungry"

And went on; "Can lose appetite like a sick person."

Takwe had listed the ways to identify a thief in the village

For the villagers have never seen or heard of a thief.

Takwe's nocturnal activities have done much to estrange

The farmers from hunters whose fields and farms were bare

Another hunting season came and passed and little changed

But the wise chief consoled them and told them not to despair

The hunters and farmers were not interested in their occupation

But the wise chief discouraged anyone from doing anything unfair

He met with all his council of elders and welcomed all propositions

To resolve the plague that was making his subjects breathe foul air.

Everything was laid out on how to sanctify

the village and stop it from falling into evil hands

The village crier was dispatched to notify

All the villagers in the four corners of the land

To honor the summons of the wise chief

Everyone in search of the truth and solace

Came anxious to see and exile the thief

Latecomers didn't have a stool in the palace.

All rituals and incantations repeated over and over

All the adults walked to the center of the courtyard

Raised both hands straight above their heads

Rubbed the middle finger thrice on a lump of wood ash

Stretched out the tongue and placed the finger

in the center of the tongue

Licked it and smacked the lips

Looked straight at the midday sun and swore

I'm not a thief

I've never seen a thief.

If I'm one

Let me shiver

Let me tremble.

Let me strutter;

Unable to eat this corn fufu.

The villagers were ready for the game; no one faltered

No one shivered, no one trembled, no one stuttered

All ate their lump of fufu; no one regurgitated

The wise chief conducted a meticolous roll call

Takwe and Taamba did not answer his call.

He saw those who wanted his downfall.

As a wise chief, he had to stand proud and tall

The wise chief was ready to go to his court hall

When he heard a commotion in the yard.

Takwe was strolling across the yard

He swore as everyone before him did

He didn't shiver, he didn't tremble,he didn't strutter

He ate his lump of corn fufu tantalizingly, he didn't regurgitate

Taamba followed, shivering and unable to raise his trembling
hands

Taamba's thighs were wet and dripping with what looked like
urine

The villagers were completely astonished

to see Taamba shiver and look demolished

But no one could utter the word thief

for they were still waiting for their chief

But their wise chief was still cautious

He waited for Taamba to be conscious

To defend himself from the allegations

That could be proven after the interrogations

The wise chief didn't like the provocations

But Takwe embarrassed Taamba with a question

"Taamba, why have you pissed on yourself ?"

Takwe asked and went on "You're a thief."

Taamba opened his mouth, it quivered and shivered

His legs and hands trembled; so he could not deliver

A speech to save him from such false accusations

Taamba could not say anything about the manipulation

Of his friend who put him in a pool to cleanse him of filth and dirt

But little did he know he was scheming for his exile or his death

"Taamba is hungry" Takwe said

"Give him corn fufu and vegetable to eat"

Takwe knew Taamba doesn't eat fufu without meat

He knew that his best friend had frostbite,

His neck was like a child with mumps; he could not bite

Even a sappy piece of meat he could not taste

Takwe lectured the elders that Tamba was a pest

That shivering, trembling and refusing food is a crime.

Taamba freezing and tongue-tied was not given time.

As it was given his close, trusted and inseparable friend

"Thief! Thief! Thief!" Takwe shouted and was joined by the villagers

Taamba, quivering, shivering,and trembling, was exiled from the village.

Takwe's slogan: "when he sees the owner," was recited by the villagers.

. . .

Takwe: The brain of a thief can never be at peace

Elders: When he sees the owner

Takwe: The heart of a thief can never be at ease

Elders: When he sees the owner

Takwe: Only a thief trembles and shivers

Elders: When he sees the owner

Takwe: A thief can become dumb and deaf or strutter

Elders When he sees the owner.

Takwe one afternoon when all villagers were on their farms

Ate bowls of corn fufu with chunks of meat from his barn

He was so happy to sing one of his revised favorite songs

Very happy that the poor folks didn't know right from wrong

A village where the wise steal

and the idiots pay the price

A village where the wise eat

The juiciest parts of a game

And the idiots eat the offals

burp and are very contented

A village where idiots like Taamba

Toil and sweat night and day

The wise like us dine and wine but

They belch and are very contented.

With idiots, life is enjoyable

Without idiots, life will be miserable

There's a common saying in the grass field that:

"The eyes and ears of a wise chief are everywhere."

The chief had informants everywhere

When Taamba left, they put things right

The wise chief had to measure and weigh

Everything about Takwe day and night

One day the villagers were summoned by the wise chief

He asked them to repeat a catch phrase " Must be a thief "

Chief: A villager who takes from the left and doesn't want the right to know

and takes from the right and doesn't want the left to-

Villagers: Must be a thief.

Chief: A villager who carries an antelope on his head

and snatches a termite from a hen feeding chi-

Villagers: Must be a thief! Must be a thief!

Chief: A villager who hears a knock on the door

and hides what he was eating under the-

Villagers: Must be a thief! Must be a thief!

Chief: A villager who is afraid of showers of rain

and is terrified by the rays of the su-

Villagers: Must be a thief! Must be a thief!

Chief: A villager who has not taken a bath because the pool is freezing

but advises his friend to bathe in the freezing poo-

Villagers: Must be a thief! Must be a thief!

Chief: A villager who crosses a bamboo bridge

and cuts the bamboo for firewoo-

Villagers: Must be a thief! Must be a thief!

Chief: A villager who takes shelter from the rain in a hut

and excretes in the hut before lea-

Villagers: Must be a thief! Must be a thief! Must be a...

When the wise chief finished his recitation

He asked his subjects to look around to see

If they can see anyone who fits that description

All the villagers turned round as if stung by a bee

Opened their mouths as if awoken from a nightmare

Stupefied by what they have all directly or indirectly marred

Instead of looking at the position, Takwe was sitting.

Blinded by the truth, they looked everywhere.

They were all afraid to see the sun setting;

Before dusk, Takwe was seen nowhere.

3. Takwe and Taamba killed their mothers

Once upon a time, Takwe and Tamba, great hunters, were haunted

They were starving and chafing; the bones in their ribs could be counted

Food and water were hard to get, life was hard, unbearable and hopeless

Their hunting fields were barren, the trees were leafless and lifeless.

Takwe and Tamba could hardly remember when they last ate twice a day

Their lips were cracked, confirming the fact that hunger has come to stay

Takwe and Taamba had the worst hunting season in their lives

The animals were wiser and smarter; very cautious with their lives

Even the animals that were idiots were not falling into deep pits

Dug by Takwe and Taamba, who were also both looking stupid

Even all idiots who slept and snored slept with one eye open

Even Taamba's dreams of better traps and meals didn't happen.

Takwe and Tamba waited for a swarm of locusts or grasshoppers in vain

Migrating birds and insects changed direction and flew to less hostile plains

Even the bats that visited the grassland had no trees to perch on on the hills

Hibernating animals that were very dormant and inactive were on their heels

Making those who wanted to harvest without sowing to count stars at night

Takwe and Taamba slept and wondered what they were not doing right.

Takwe and Taamba went ferreting for mushrooms to keep busy

Things that were done by women and children were not even easy

It was as if even common mushrooms had migrated to foreign lands.

Hunger had made contours on their bodies, shrinking their legs and hands

Their intestines were wriggling, wrinkling and coiling and no more grumbled

Taamba stood up, chewed dry bones, got dizzy, lost his step and stumbled.

Takwe started a queer conversation one day.

"Living too old on earth is a problem."

"Like my old mother; she is a big problem,"Taamba said angrily

"Old people are useless on earth," Takwe continued.

"Like my old mother; she is very useless" Taamba said fuming

"Old people eat without working" Takwe said

"Like my old mother;" Taamba said whining and added

"She eats too much without working"

Takwe and Taamba were hungrier and angrier each passing day

They brainstormed but couldn't agree on ways to make their mothers pay

For the lumps of corn fufu and chunks of meat, they ate when life was good

Taamba was wondering how his mother was still happy eating soured food

The toothless mother still cracked hard, dry bones when life was unbearable

He said to himself, "This trend of wayward life is irritating and miserable."

Takwe and Taamba had gone for another fruitless hunting expedition

It was as if the foolish animals wanted to put them in a cross-termination

Takwe and Taamba were falling into their own traps instead of the animals

The animals made what was abnormal normal and the formal, informal

Taamba, in desperation while furiously chasing a rat, fell into a pit in the woods.

Takwe pulled him out and brushed his bruises and licked the bleeding wounds.

Takwe looking at his frustrated and dejected friend, said casually

"If an old woman fell in a pit, I won't pull her out."

"Like my old, toothless, useless mother," Taamba said angrily.

"Only idiots fall in pits; wise women can't," Takwe said wryly.

"Like my worthless old mother" Taamba snapped in furiously

Your mother is old but wise and smart."

"Wise and smart in eating all my meat and leaving bones for me."

"If she falls in a spit and dies, will you not regret it?"

"Regret! Not me. "

"What if she drowns in a deep river?"

"Better; I won't see her corpse."

Tamba was not frustrated with the fruitless hunt but with the mother

So, it was not surprising that he accepted Takwe's plan to murder

"If we kill for food, it's not bad; killing to survive is not an abomination."

"Yap" Takwe said,"It won't be an abomination but a benediction."

"Yap" Taamba said "Mothers who want their children to eat and grow

should continue to scratch like hens when the earth is hard as a rock."

To make their children live a happy life even when the sky is red, not blue.

Takwe said: "Tomorrow we must chase this wind that brings bad luck."

Takwe enjoyed the argument coming from his hungry starving friend

Who had not yet realized that such a proposal could only come from a fiend

And pretended as if he was not the one who brought up such an abomination

But still made his feeble-minded friend Taamba to believe it 'll be a benediction.

Taamba was hungry, worried, but very eager to have beef no matter the source

But didn't realize his trusted companion was leading him on the wrong course.

. . .

"It won't be good for you to see me killing my mother

And it won't be good for me to see you killing your mother."

Takwe started giving the plans on how the killings will be done

"But it will be a good thing; this benediction is better before dawn

"Good idea! Takwe, wise decision" Taamba exclaimed.

Takwe continued. "I'll slaughter my mother at the top of the stream

You slay yours at the bottom when you see blood flowing down stream

"Good idea! Takwe, wise decision." Taamba exclaimed again

The Benediction Day came; Takwe took his mother to the top of the stream

Taamba tied dragged and carted his mother to the bottom of the stream

Taamba, have you seen blood flowing and whirling in the stream ?"

Takwe shouted from the top of the stream

"Yes! Yes!" Taamba shouted excitedly

"How is the stream?" Takwe asked

"So much blood! So much blood flowing and whirling"

Taamba said excitedly and continued "Easy hunting, Takwe."

Taamba immediately butchered his own mother as in the plot

Put the chunks and slices in the pot that was set on a tripod

And cooked a delicious porridge just like his mother used to cook

Takwe, with a watering mouth full of saliva, came to share the food

Taamba ate greedily in a way no hunter has ever eaten before

They both emptied their bowls, licked their fingers and took more.

Takwe and Taamba went upstream to eat Takwe's meal

But they noticed that the fire under the tripod was so mean.

Taamba went on his knees and blew the fire with all his strength

Takwe also went on his knees and blew until he ran out of breath

"Let's put down the pot and eat," Takwe said

"It's too early. Not yet well cooked," Tamba replied

" I know my mother. Let's put it down."

"Let's wait; let me add more wood."

"Let's eat now. I know why."

"Let me add more wood and kindle longer."

At midday, Tamba, who was very hungry, put down the pot

At the top, he found a few slices of meat and a few bones

The second layer was hard hides and barks and red stones

"What am I seeing? Tamba cried

"I warned you. You put the pot too long on the fire."

"I wanted to cook it well as I did with my mother's..."

"My mother is not your mother, I warned you"

Takwe added" The longer she is cooked, the harder she becomes."

"I want to taste your mother's beef. I want to eat and..."

"Let's eat fast, anything can happen."

Takwe shared the little slices of beef and bones in the pot

And told Taamba that it's better to eat the slices of beef hot

Because the few slices found can also harden into stones

Taamba believed what he heard that beef could turn to bones

Especially If it is the beef of a mother heartless like a stone

Weeks later, Taamba was hungry and looked miserable

But Takwe, who was healthy, said Taamba was adorable

And a brave, courageous friend who is not only caring but selfless.

So, he needed his company because they were both motherless

To someone who has not eaten, what Takwe said was senseless

Taamba's friend was healthier and merrier as if nothing had changed

To Taamba, who was starving, chaffing and pale this was very strange.

Taamba, hunting in the forest one day, heard a strange song

Takwe blew his flute merrily dancing, singing so loud and long

"Someone in a distant past, in a distant land

Because of hunger roasted his mother and ate

But was still dying of hunger and starvation.

Later became so envious of someone else's mother

Only an idiot can slaughter the mother for food

the wise will want their mothers to live forever.

Takwe told Taamba it was a song in a distant land beyond the skies.

And a very long, long time ago in a distant land where no baby cries.

Taamba believed his close friend, who knew and narrated many stories

But he was still wondering how Takwe had regular tasteful porridge

In his house, any time they returned hungrily and food was out of reach

Taamba, the brave hunter, was poor, while Takwe, a weak hunter, was rich.

Takwe decided one day to tell Taamba the origin of his flute

"This flute that I made from a hollow reed from the stream

Where I slew my mother makes me healthy and I dream

That our huntings one day will be fruitful and we'll be happy

We can be hungry today but tomorrow our meals will be sappy

That's why in my songs, I mention Mama Mama several times

Sending them a lovely message that what we did was not a crime."

Taamba started enjoying the melodious and enchanting flute

He started dreaming of going to the stream to curve his own flute

With the hope of being happy, healthy and jovial like his companion

And dreaming of going to where he slew his mother for a family reunion

Through the blood, he spilled in the stream to chase away the hunger

Takwe continued singing each day, but this could not subdue his anger

Without a mother, Taamba was living in his own hut like an insane monger.

Takwe's flute echoed in the hills and valleys and caves

Peep, peep, peep, tamara, mamatarama, beep pom

Peep , peep , peep, tamara, mamatarama, beep pom

Every afternoon making the birds tweet and cuckoo

To Takwe, the flute made life sweet and enjoyable

But to Taamba, it made him remorseful and miserable.

.   .   .

Takwe and Taamba came back home one day life was still rough

Takwe scratched his head several times and cracked a dry cough

He looked worried with a cloud of sadness all over his weary face

Taamba noticed that something was wrong or not in the right place

Taamba was climbing the hill leading to Takwe's hut on a terrace

And heard:

"Mama !Mama! Rush and hide in the ceiling

Mama! Mama! Rush and hide in the ceiling

Mama! mama! Rush and hide in the ceiling!"

Taamba, surprised by what he heard, sprang and galloped up the hill

Takwe tried to spring, tried to gallop, tried to run but had weak heels

Taamba galloped with anger, skipped and climbed uphill without a stop

Enraged, eyes hot as fire; he heard Takwe yelling as he reached the top

"Mama hide! Taamba'll kill you.

Mama hide! Taamba'll kill you.

Mama hide !Taamba'll kill you."

· · ·

Taamba sprang and jumped; he was running out of breath.

Behold, he saw Takwe's old mother escaping from death

He grabbed her by the neck, straggled and knocked her dead

Takwe saw his mother tortured; he saw her died

And for the first time, he grumbled, and he cried

He would have defended her, but he was not strong

He thought he was right and Taamba was wrong

Because he didn't see Taamba kill his own mother

Taamba thinks only of his stomach and doesn't bother

He said to himself.

Taamba wasted no time, for hunger was tearing him into pieces

He butchered the carcass into reasonable chunks and slices

And put them hurriedly in a pot on Takwe's mother's old heart

The pot was not bubbling well, so he added wood underneath

Not long Taamba started swallowing saliva and smacking his lips

While Takwe had a hacking cough. He scratched his itchy eyelids

And continued groaning, sipping, sobbing and wiping hot tears

His eyes were piercing and burning as if hit with poisoned spears

Takwe was dreaming of the camwood he threw in the stream

To deceive Taamba that he had butchered his mother

And foolish Taamba believed him.

He was dreaming of the hides, barks and stones he put in the pot

To deceive Taamba that his mother's beef turned into barks and stones

And foolishTaamba believed him.

Taamba was dreaming of his mother hiding in the ceiling

Mocking at an idiot who killed his mother because of hunger

But few days later was starving and dying of the same hunger

He was dreaming of his mother praising him as the best child on earth.

My mother, my flute, betrayed me. Taamba said to himself.

The flute that I made betrayed me. Mother, my flute betrayed me

My mother, my flute betrayed me. It's because of my flute

Taamba was embarrassed to see Takwe shed tears for the first time

He asked "Why are you crying, Takwe?"

"The smoke is itching my eyes" Takwe replied, still wiping tears.

4. Takwe, the greatest groundnut farmer

A Long time ago, in a village in the grass field, there lived a Takwe

One season he told the villagers that he will be the greatest farmer

But everyone knew that he was an idler, lazy, and was so queer

He made bets with wealthy farmers who said he was a lazy farmer

Takwe showed his palm and said :"Bet here! Bet here ! Bet here!"

Jokingly and mockingly, some wealthy groundnut farmers betted

To give him a basket of groundnut if he can harvest one basket

Takwe was seen every evening with a hoe and a machete

Announcing his return from his farm with a work song

.   .   .

Nothing is good as hard work

Hard Work brings a good harvest

A good harvest brings smiles

Nothing is as go as hard work

I'm the greatest farmer in this village

Idlers will die of jealousy

The villagers were bored listening to the same song morning and evening

The song was not only melodious, but it also made so much sense

They knew that the idler and vagabond had copied it from a praise singer

They listened and wondered why it should be Takwe giving busy farmers

Lessons on how to hold a hoe and telling them the merits of hard work

The villagers jeered and mocked the Takwe

They said idlers and tricksters can't be harvesters

But Takwe licked the soil and pointed at the sky

And said: "My heap of groundnut will touch the sky."

Even Takwe's wife was doubting what the husband was hatching

But Takwe assured her that he had tilled a large farm far away

Because of slash-and-burning farming, he had crossed seven rivers

He said only lazy farmers work with their wives on the same farms

He asked the wife to relax at home and enjoy the fruits of a hard-working husband

The Planting season came and the villagers went to their farms early

They went to the farms at cock crow and came when fowls were roosting

Takwe asked his wife to prepare three calabashes raw, boiled and fried

groundnuts; he went to the forest and ate each day for a whole week

Drank fresh water spurting from a spring and cleared his cracked voice and sang:

Oh, sweet groundnuts!

Where did you come from?

Raw, you taste sweet

Boiled, you taste sweet

Fried, you taste sweet

sweeter than nectar

That bees suck

Sweeter than honey

that bees produce

Easier to tap than honey

Easier to tap than wine

Sweet all the times

and on all occasion

Oh, sweet groundnut!

Where did you come from?

He went and drank fresh water from the spring and relaxed till sunset

And came back home with a hoe on his shoulder, looking more upset

Than farmers who toiled the whole season with hard callous hands

And still fought pestering weeds, insects and birds on their farmlands

Under intense heat and torrential rains, without bragging and singing

Takwe, every evening even without moonlight, went round alone singing:

Nothing is good as hard work

Hard Work brings a good harvest

A good harvest brings smiles

Nothing is good as hard work

I am the greatest farmer in this village

Idlers will die of jealousy

Takwe's wife insisted and persisted in going and harvest the groundnuts

He hit his chest proudly and said that he tilled and sowed alone

So as a hard-working husband, he had to harvest the yields alone

He asked his wife to cross her legs leisurely like on their honeymoon

And enjoy the fruits of a busy, caring, loving and hard-working husband.

The harvest season came; the farmers were busy from cock crow hustling

For the first time, Takwe's granaries were filled with bags of groundnuts

After many years of marriage, the wife was the happiest in the village

The villages were losing their bets and paying the bags of groundnuts

Many paid grudgingly and were regretting why they made such bets

Takwe hit his chest proudly and went around singing loudly

This time he was accompanied by his wife, who sang the chorus

Wise farmers work on rich soil

Foolish farmers work on poor soil

Wise farmers get rich every year

Foolish farmers get poor every year

When the wise laugh; the idiots cry

One day Takwe came as usual to the farm to carry his yields

He was surprised to meet a robust man on the farm before dawn.

He greeted and had no answer; he shouted and had no answer

He decided to slap this intruder where he was reaping

He slapped with his right hand and the hand got stuck

He threatened "My left hand is dangerous and deadly."

He gave another deadly slap, but it also got stuck

He threatened; My kicks are poisonous and deadly."

He went on,"Don't let me kick you."

No reply was given. So he kicked and the right leg got stuck.

He threatened again; "My left leg is very wicked."

He insisted: "If it touches you, you will regret why you were born."

He put all his strength in the kick but it also got stuck

Takwe is panting and sweating despite the chilly morning

Swung to the left and to the right hoping to get loose

At sunrise, he discovered he was glued on a man-shape trap

He thought of knocking the scarecrow with his head to be free

When he saw Taamba taking shortcuts to his farm

Takwe started swinging to the left and right, singing.

You swing to the left

You swing to the right

Sweet groundnut farm

You move up; you move down

Sweet groundnut farm

Sweet for those who work hard

Sweet groundnut farm.

Perplexed, Taamba raised his hands in the air in astonishment

To see his friend so early swinging and dancing on the chief's farm

Takwe said nothing and continued singing and enjoying the game

Taamba begged to be allowed to swing, sing and dance like him

Takwe said it was a practice for those to dance for the chief

To choose the best dancer as a suitor for her daughter, the princess.

Taamba put his hoe down and went on his knees, bowed and begged

Takwe reluctantly accepted to be pulled down to give his friend a chance

Taamba pulled the legs and hands of Takwe with so much force

And slapped and kicked the motionless man forcefully

His hands and legs got glued as they were with Takwe.

Taamba's coarse, cracked voice echoed in the valleys below

As he sang, swung and danced to the left and then to the right

He sang, swung and danced up and down, forward and backwards

Got absorbed and ecstatic and thanked Takwe for the opportunity

He coughed and cleared his throat and could sing better now

And was about to yell and shout with joy to do it for the fifth time

When Takwe saw the chief and his bodyguards marching on

Takwe ran and bowed and clapped his hand three times

And said: chief! Chief! Chief! I 've caught your groundnut thief."

And added "He is no other than Taamba, your avowed enemy."

The chief shouted: "Haba! Haba! Haba! Tamba"

And added furiously: You steal my fowls, goats and sheep

And now you have stolen my bags of groundnuts."

The chief didn't wait for the council of elders to sanction

Taamba was sent into exile out of the grass field for seven seasons.

Takwe was rewarded with the rest of the bags of groundnuts

The bodyguards carried the bags of groundnuts to add to his
high heap

That evening Takwe and his wife went around the village singing
and dancing.

Wise farmers work on rich soil

Foolish farmers work on poor soil

Wise farmers get rich every year

Foolish farmers get poor every year

When the wise laugh; the idiots cry

Takwe didn't go to his field to start tilling the soil for planting

He said good farmers know when to till, sow and harvest

But idiots toil and sweat under the sun and are drenched in
the rain

And still, look as pale as an eye of a broom and weaker than
an eye

The wise are strong and healthy because they eat well and sleep
well.

Hard-working farmers argued that Takwe only sings after a
tasteful meal

They argued hard work is preferable to melodious songs from
loafers

But the song was on every lip; especially on the lips of
babysitters

As if it was the only song that could lull a nagging baby to sleep.

They have inserted the word 'babysitter' in their own version

Nothing is good as hard work

Hard Work brings a good harvest

A good harvest brings smiles

Nothing is good as hard work

I'm the greatest babysitter in the grass field

Idlers will die of jealousy.

Young boys and girls sang the songs to scare birds from their farms

And grains of maize, guinea corn and millet were spared that season.

"If you touch me; I'll say what you did to Taamba"

Takwe's wife shouted after a dispute

"If you look at me again with the corner of your eye, I'll...

I'm a good wife. I don't talk like other women."

"SSSH! SSSHYI ! SSHYI" Takwe put his finger on his lip.

Pleading with the eyes of a dove for the wife to shut her lips.

As it was commonly said in that village:1

"Opened the hens's nesting boxes in broad moonlight."

What was hidden from the villagers was known to all

Takwe source of heaps of groundnuts was known to all

The remaining bags were taken to the village hall

To be shared with the hungry poor who refused to mar

Their reputation and dignity in times of hardship.

Takwe was exiled from the village for seven seasons

And poor Taamba, who was sentenced for no reason

Was re-integrated in the village after the hunting season.

The council of elders sentenced Takwe the croak

To climb seven hills and cross seven streams

And until after seven seasons, should not dream

Of returning to the village or having any contact

With anyone in the village, either directly or indirectly

He was ordered to clean his tongue with a splitter

of bamboo and threw over his head and didn't look back.

The day Taakwe was sent into exile came

The villagers thronged both sides of the road

To see Takwe, the idler, carry his shameful load

His once-bright eyes looked like those of a toad.

The villagers croaked, grunted, mocked and booed

        · · ·

Nothing is bad as laziness

Laziness brings a bad harvest

A bad harvest brings sorrow

Nothing is as bad as laziness

Takwe is the laziest farmer in the grass field.

5. Taamba dies in a wildfire contest

A long time ago, Takwe and Taamba

had fiefs of hunting fields in the grassland

Takwe's hunting fief was in the east of Mamba

This field was surrounded by vast farmlands.

Taamba had the hilly fields in the west of Teraba

The hills where only brave hunters go at night.

There were so many dos and don'ts before,

the bushes were burnt; which must be done right

So, the owner of each hunting field, therefore

Performed specific rituals before midnight.

This is one of the rituals that was often recited:

Hunters of the hills and valleys. Let's be cautious

The big, the small, the brave, the courageous.

Hunting brings us together; hunting unites us.

Let the big and the small play their roles.

Let the brave and courageous play their roles.

In the end, let the big or small have an equal share

Let the brave or courageous have an equal share

So wildfire spirits as we pour this wine and blood

Bless our weapons ignite our fire and do good

Bless our hands and feet to hunt well.

Let us do well and eat well in this world.

Let those who came clean go back clean.

Let those who came dirty also go back clean.

Takwe, a few seasons later, said that he was bored

with the monotonous old hunting traditions.

He said hunting in the grassland was no more

exciting, because hunters reject new conditions

He said it was boring going for a hunting

expedition, they already knew what was hurting.

He said the villagers knew that Taamba

with his brute force caught all the big games.

He was to turn things to catch the big games

instead of rodents and doing the sharing;

while Taamba can rest and watch his bravery

and do the sharing and get the complaints

from insatiable folks who hardly live their beds.

He, Takwe, had been having from catchers

of rodents, calves, cobs and harmless birds.

So he started a conversation on the eve of the launch

"Brave hunters do brave things "

"Like what?" Taamba asked

"Like standing in the middle of a burning bush."

"No hunter can do that."

"I can do it."

You can't."

"I can"

" I'm braver than you. I can do more than you."

Taamba said, hitting his chest proudly.

Taamba was ready for any extraordinary adventures

where bravery, strength and courage were put to test.

The feat was: a hunter will stand in the heart of his treasure

until every blade of grass is razed and made as if it's just a jest

Inhaling baskets of smoke, feeling the intense heat and pressure

and remain calm without touching, mending any fissure

At the end of the jest, come out singing with great pleasure.

"Yap!" Tamba shouted excitedly

"Something new! Captivating reserved for the brave like me."

Taamba wanted to be the first to show his power and bravery

But Takwe pleaded to be the first to show his grit and bravery

Taamba accepted when Takwe gave him a sappy piece of meat

Takwe assured him that after the hunt, they would never lack meat.

The day for the extraordinary feat came;

Takwe walked proudly, ready for the game.

Made his incantations and said:

This rich bush belongs to me

So, no amount of fire can kill me

Animals living in my bush will die

It's my bush.It's my bush .I can't die

Takwe went to the center of his burning bush boldly

Through a passage that was getting narrower and deadly

From all the four corners leaving a narrow corridor

He climbed to the top of his hut and smiled broadly

He watched Tamba kindling the smoky corridor

"Taamba, are you seeing me standing proud and tall."

"I'm seeing you, oh Takwe."

"Simple.That's how you'll…"

"Yes! Yes! I'll do…."

Before he finished, the fire went wild

rumbling howling, rustling, hustling

A whirlwind spun the flames higher and higher

The insects fleeing to safety higher and higher

Scavengers fighting and scrambling to hire

the fleeing insects into their homes safe from fire

As the resisting scrubs and logs were still glowing

Taamba emerged from the ashes ,grinning

"Hurray! Hurray! Hurray! Oyee! Oyee! Oyee!

Takwe shouted, throwing hot ashes in the air

Taamba wiped his eyes and brushed his hair

From the hot, smoky aches but could not hear

He was tiptoeing to the burnt hut following a lair

"Don't go that way," Takwe shouted and continued

"I excreted that way. The fetor can kill."

Taamba blocked his nostrils and made an upturn

With fangs opened widely

He listened to Takwe reverently.

"It was very exciting and enthralling"

Takwe said after hiccups passionately

"I inhaled smoke and my red, brave eyes refused to weep

And when I exhaled it, I saw where the sun goes to sleep

I inhaled and exhaled again. I saw a pale, yellow moon weeping

And I sat on a throne; I saw the sun and the stars eating and sipping;

What looked like nectar, sweeter than honey. It's real. I wasn't dreaming."

Takwe raised a finger and pointed at the sun above their heads, beaming

They went round tracking and sniffing all holes

Taamba caught more animals than he could hold

Takwe went around picking dead rodents and insects

He was unable to dig holes but knew how to select

The biggest games without giving any good reason

Taamba didn't complain because he did that every season.

That night Taamba was dreaming of the quiet world

Takwe painted that the sun, stars and moon are well

The sun, moon and stars dine and wine without halting

While hunger gnawed their intestines without quitting

He was ready to show his boldness and courage

To have all the haunches and a pot of porridge

That Takwe promised if he respected their pact

Then no hunter would enter another's hunting park.

The sun for the endurance test was ready for what will happen

Taamba trudged and mounted to the top of his hut in the center

And watched how Takwe completed a corridor that was left open

For him to walk through as the flames were rushing to the epicenter

It was a hot sunny and windy day, so the fire went wild

A roaring fire razed all turfs, shaving all grasses low

And launched an assault on anything in the field

From behind and before, from above and below

The flames twisted, mauled, turned and tore

Taamba saw fire burnt and went above the law

It was not just a game but an announced war

Taamba, overwhelmed, shouted in agony

"Oh Takwe! How should I stand ?"

"Just stand as I stood" Takwe replied

"Oh! Oh! How! Should I stand?"

"Just stand as I stood" Takwe repeated.

The birds swung, weaved and dived in the smoke

scrambling and snatching desperate insects fleeing

and were booing, beeping and mocking and messing

On the head of Taamba, who was haunted;

Wonder why Taamba, the great hunter

was screaming, yelling and wailing

like a bull shot in the head by a hunter

When birds could dive, float and hunt

Enjoying the fun of a see-saw

Reaping where they didn't sow.

Taamba could not blink, the fire was chewing him raw

The fire pierced right into the heart of his heart; he was shot

He moaned, snatching his teeth, blood dripping from his jaw

As flames of death wrapped and mutilated him on the spot

Takwe skipped, hopped and danced triumphantly

Avoiding hotspots, he walked jiggly and stealthily

He chuckled, hitting Taamba's roasted fangs and said:

Tamba, you thought you were powerful; stand and walk

Tamba, you thought you were brave; stand and walk

Only idiots like you will foolishly want to fight with fire

The wise like me always have another way to escape the fire

I dug a deep hole to hide from the ravaging flames

Taamba, when will idiots like you accept the blames

Foolish Taamba stand up, walk, and talk again

You gave your precious life for a cheap bargain

He peeled Taamba's skin and nailed it on his wall

Chopped the beef, boiled some roasted and baked

Some, for weeks, he relaxed and enjoyed the windfall

He was happy he had his revenge and had enough

To eat for a season and have no strong rival around.

But after some time, he noticed something very strange

Taamba's skin got fresher and fresher and healing fast

He spat on the skin three times tfu! tfu! tfu! and said

"Taamba, you can't come back to life

My mother, whom you killed, didn't come back

So, you can't come back to life."

He spat three times tfu, tfu, tfu again

And went hunting on his large fields

Taamba's skin pinned on the wall

Continued to germinate each day

Takwe continued to spit tfu tfu tfu

Cursed and insulted Taamba's skin

whenever he saw any changes.

One day, Takwe came from his field

And met the ugliest surprise of his life

He met Taamba lurching to kill him

He ran away, pleading with his legs

"My legs, what I have eaten

And have not given you?

Take me away fast"

Takwe's legs obeyed and flew him out of the Teraba hills

Hungry Taamba could not run fast on his feeble heels

So, he went back to eat and practice new hunting skills.